THE LAST
Sherlock
Holmes
STORY

Michael Dibdin

Retold by
Rosalie Kerr

OXFORD UNIVERSITY PRESS

Oxford University Press
Great Clarendon Street, Oxford OX2 6DP

Oxford New York
Athens Auckland Bangkok Bogota Bombay
Buenos Aires Calcutta Cape Town Dar es Salaam Delhi
Florence Hong Kong Istanbul Karachi Kuala Lumpur
Madras Madrid Melbourne Mexico City Nairobi
Paris Singapore Taipei Tokyo Toronto Warsaw

and associated companies in
Berlin Ibadan

OXFORD and OXFORD ENGLISH
are trade marks of Oxford University Press

ISBN 0 19 421675 6

Original edition © Michael Dibdin 1978
First published by Jonathan Cape Ltd 1978
This simplified edition © Oxford University Press 1995

First published 1995
Fourth impression 1997

Illustrated by Paul Dickinson

Typeset by Wyvern Typesetting Ltd, Bristol
Printed in England by
Clays Ltd, St Ives plc

Foreword

Many people enjoy Sir Arthur Conan Doyle's stories about the famous detective, Sherlock Holmes, and his friend, Dr Watson. But who now remembers that Holmes and Watson were real people? Everyone has forgotten that they lived before Conan Doyle gave them life in his books.

Dr Watson died in 1926. He was seventy-three. He left behind him a locked box, and orders that it must not be opened for fifty years.

For fifty years the box lay hidden in a dark room below a bank. Years came and went, and the world changed in a thousand ways.

In 1976 the box was opened. It contained a packet of papers. They tell a terrible story. Some people say it cannot be true. They say Watson was lying, or that he was sick when he wrote it. After so many years we cannot be sure. We have checked all the facts that we can. All we know is that the story could be true. It is possible. We think it is probable. Now you must read it and decide for yourself.

THE EDITORS

Re: Sherlock Holmes
Not to be opened
until 1976
Dr Watson.

In 1976 the box was opened. It contained a packet of papers.

Introduction

How well my friend Arthur Conan Doyle would tell this story! How exciting and interesting he would make it. I cannot do that. I am no writer. I have been a doctor and a soldier. All I can do is make my report.

But who will read my words? What will the world be like in 1976? Perhaps by then nobody will know the names of Sherlock Holmes and Jack the Ripper. Perhaps all Conan Doyle's wonderful stories will be forgotten. There is so much to explain. I must ask my reader to be patient!

I had known and worked with Sherlock Holmes for almost four years when I first met Arthur Conan Doyle – ACD I always called him. Like me, he was a doctor, and we quickly became good friends. He told me amusing stories of hospital life, and I told him about my life as an army doctor in Afghanistan.

I often talked to him about Sherlock Holmes. At that time most people had never heard of him. Only the police and some criminals knew what a great detective he was. ACD seemed to enjoy my stories very much. He was never too tired to hear about another of Holmes's cases.

We met many times and enjoyed many good dinners together before I realized that ACD had a special interest in Holmes. He wanted to be a writer, and had already enjoyed a little success. Now he wanted to write about Holmes, using the facts of a real case, but adding his own ideas to the story. I found this an excellent idea. I was happy to think that my dear friend would become famous.

I explained the plan to Holmes. He listened in silence, his pipe in his hand. Then he said, 'Can he write, this friend of yours? Can he tell a true story? Does he understand the difference between facts and lies?'

'I think so,' I said. 'He has just begun to write, but already he is becoming fashionable.'

'Fashionable!' Holmes said coldly. 'How can it interest me that he is fashionable? Can a fashionable writer have a serious interest in the facts of one of my cases?'

I could not reply. Holmes sat silently, looking into the fire. At last he said, 'Well, he may try. Let him do what he can. You may send him your notes on the Hope case, Watson.'

I wrote to ACD the next day, and he began work on the story. He called it *A Study in Scarlet*. When it appeared in the shops, I hurried out to buy it, and then sat for hours in a park reading it. The story was excellent – fast-moving, exciting and clever. I ran back to Baker Street. I could not wait to give the book to Holmes.

He looked up quickly as I entered the room.

'You're late, Watson,' he said. 'Were you ashamed to come here with that book in your hand?'

'Ashamed, Holmes?' I cried. 'No! ACD has done well. I see you have read it. Why don't you like it?'

I was soon sorry that I had spoken.

'Like it? It is rubbish, wild and fantastic rubbish. He has been careless with the facts, added all kinds of unnecessary lies, and made the most stupid mistakes.'

When the book appeared in the shops, I hurried out to buy it.

'But Holmes . . .'

'I wonder what kind of doctor he is. I am sorry for his patients. I would not be surprised to hear that he had cut off a man's leg because the man had a stomach ache. He is clearly not interested in facts.'

'Holmes,' I said as calmly as I could, 'a writer does not just report facts. He must make sure that the story is interesting to read. I am sure you understand that.'

Holmes smiled at me sweetly.

'My dear fellow,' he said. 'I forget. You know all about fine writing. How stupid of me to worry about a few careless mistakes! But your friend Mr Doyle has shown that he does not understand how important my work is. He thinks that the criminals I fight against are stupid, miserable little beings. They are not. I fight against evil itself. He has failed to understand that. The book is worthless. Away with it, and with your friend the writer!'

I wondered what to say to ACD, but there was no need to worry. *A Study in Scarlet* was not a success, and he began to write about other things. Several years later he decided to write about Holmes again, but at that time I had other things to think about. I had fallen in love with Miss Mary Morstan. When she agreed to become my wife, I hurried to tell Holmes. I was full of happiness.

I can still hear the cold surprise in his voice as he said, 'I cannot pretend to be happy about this.'

This hurt me terribly, but I tried to laugh.

'Well, Holmes,' I said, 'I hope you won't be too lonely when

I had fallen in love with Miss Mary Morstan.

I go home to my wife.'

A shadow passed over his face.

'Oh no, Watson,' he said. 'I still have my cocaine-bottle.'

Was he asking me for help? Was it still possible, then, to save him? Perhaps. In my heart I know only that my dear friend needed me, and that I failed him.

The first murders

Sherlock Holmes became a detective in 1877, four years before I met him. At first he enjoyed every case, but soon he began to find the work easy. Ten years later he was famous, but he was unhappy and bored.

'The modern criminal is so painfully slow and stupid,' he often said. 'I need an interesting case, Watson, one which will make me think. Are there no clever thieves or murderers in the world these days?'

It is dangerous for a very intelligent man like Holmes to become bored. Some days he grew violent and once he shot several bullets into the walls of his room. He also began to use cocaine.

Does my reader know about cocaine, I wonder? Perhaps it is no longer used in the world of 1976. It is a useful medicine, and doctors rightly give it to patients who are in pain. But Holmes had no disease of the body. He used cocaine as a drug, because he enjoyed it. It made the long days seem more exciting. Soon he needed it every day, and could not live without it.

I told him to stop, but he only laughed at me. 'My dear fellow, I wish I could! Only bring me an interesting case, a difficult problem, and I shall forget my cocaine!'

One day in 1888 a note arrived from Scotland Yard. When Holmes opened it, he laughed and jumped to his feet.

'Inspector Lestrade wishes to see me,' he said. 'The police

need my help, Watson. You know, of course, that someone is murdering women in Whitechapel?'

'Of course,' I replied. 'The newspapers are full of it. Three women are dead, and the police seem unable to find the killer. Everybody knows this. Life is cheap on the streets of Whitechapel for women of that kind. What can interest you in their miserable deaths?'

'It is an extraordinary case, Watson,' Holmes cried. 'I have been studying it. I knew the police would need my help. Shall I tell you the facts?'

'Please do!' I said. Was this going to be one of Sherlock Holmes's great cases? I hoped that at last he had found something to interest him.

'The women who died were poor, and neither young nor beautiful,' he told me. 'So they were not killed for money or for love. Why were they killed? That is one mystery. There is another. Each woman was killed with a knife. The word "killed", Watson, cannot describe the violent and terrible ways in which they were murdered. They were cut up like meat. The stomach of one was opened, the head of another almost cut from her body. But this is not the worst. There are things that even the newspapers will not describe.'

He showed me a doctor's report on one of the bodies. As I read it, a sick feeling came over me.

'What man could do this?' I asked. 'What possible reason could he have to do this to a woman? Why, Holmes, why?'

He smiled coolly at me.

'Why indeed? That is the real interest of this case. In

themselves, these deaths are not important. Women like that are murdered every week. But why does this killer cut them up? Why rip the bodies to pieces with a knife? That is the question which makes this case so exciting!'

If anyone can stop these terrible murders, Holmes is that man, I thought. This case could become his greatest success.

At that moment somebody knocked at the door.

'Ah, come in, Inspector,' Holmes said. 'I understand you have finally decided to ask me to help you catch this Whitechapel murderer.'

Inspector Lestrade did not look very pleased. 'Not at all, Mr Holmes,' he said. 'I was just passing Baker Street, and I know you find these cases interesting.'

'How kind!' Holmes said. 'Please tell us. When did you arrest the killer? I am a little sad, I must say, to find that you have done it all without me.'

'We haven't arrested anyone yet,' Lestrade said, 'but I am very hopeful, Mr Holmes. You see, I have in my pocket a letter from the killer himself.'

The smile left Holmes's face. He was suddenly serious.

'May I see the letter?' he asked.

It was written in red, and the name at the bottom was 'Jack the Ripper'. I still remember something of what it said:

I love my work. My knife is nice and ready for the next job. I can't wait to rip again.

Holmes turned to Lestrade. 'What are you doing to stop this murderer?' he asked. 'It is clear that he will kill again very soon.'

'May I see the letter?' Holmes asked.

'Every extra policeman that we have will be in Whitechapel at night,' Lestrade said. 'And we have a little surprise for Jack the Ripper.' He looked at us importantly. 'Some of our best and bravest policemen will be dressed in women's clothes,' he said. 'We will stop at nothing to catch this criminal.'

There was a moment's silence. Then Holmes and I looked at one another and we both began to laugh. We could not stop.

Lestrade turned very red. 'I see you are amused by murder,' he said. 'You do not wish to work with us. Well, I am a busy man. I must leave you. Goodbye, Mr Holmes. Goodbye, doctor.'

Holmes stopped laughing immediately.

'Inspector,' he said, 'I want very much to work with you. Let us meet this afternoon to discuss our plans.'

This made Lestrade much happier.

When he had left, I said to Holmes, 'You have laughed at the police, but what ideas do you have about these crimes? Who do you think the murderer is?'

'I do not know who he is, Watson,' he told me, 'but I believe I know what kind of man he is. He is far too intelligent, too extraordinary a killer for our good friend Lestrade and his policemen in dresses to catch. No, he shall be mine. He is the criminal that I have waited for. To destroy him will be the greatest success of my life. I dream of it, Watson! I must destroy him! I cannot fail!'

He was shaking with excitement. I had never seen him like this before.

That afternoon he went to Scotland Yard. When he came home, he was very quiet. Next day he appeared dressed in old, dirty clothes.

'I am going to Whitechapel,' he told me. 'As you know, I have rooms in several parts of London. For the next three days I shall live among the poor people of Whitechapel. Nobody will know who I am. I shall talk to them and listen to everything that they tell me.'

'May I come with you?' I asked, but he said, 'No, Watson, you may not. If there is a murder, I shall send for you. I shall need your help, old fellow, have no fear of that!'

I spent a lonely evening in Baker Street. I was asleep when, at half past two in the morning, a cab arrived to take me to

Whitechapel. Another woman had met a violent death.

As I travelled through the dark, empty streets, London seemed a strange and ghostly place – it lay there like the body of a great animal, not sleeping but dead.

The driver took me east, towards the poorest parts of the city. He stopped in a narrow lane off Leadenhall Street. I saw a group of policemen standing under a light, and went up to them. Holmes was not there, but I was introduced to the police doctor. He offered to show me the body.

'I know you are a doctor,' he said, 'but I must warn you. You have never seen anything like this before.'

He led me to a dark corner, where something lay covered on the ground. He held up a light for me to see and pulled back the cover.

No words can describe the awfulness of what I saw then. For a moment my head felt light, I began to shake and was afraid I would fall. The thing on the ground had been a woman, but it was not a woman now. It was no more than blood and meat, cut open and ripped up with a terrible, unnatural violence. I knew now why the killer called himself Jack the Ripper.

The doctor covered the body, and I walked back to the group of policemen.

'Have you seen Mr Holmes?' I asked one of them.

'Oh yes, sir,' he said. 'He was here with Inspector Lestrade. They came straight from the other murder.'

'The other murder!' I cried. 'Has there been more than one murder tonight?'

'Why yes, sir. Did you not know?'

At that moment I heard the sounds of a horse coming into the lane, and a cab appeared.

'Get in, Watson!' a voice shouted, and Holmes helped me into the cab.

'He has escaped,' he told me. 'We followed him, but we have lost him.' His face was sad and tired. 'I want to show you something interesting. Then we can go home.'

The cab took us to a dark and dirty yard.

'The first woman died here,' Holmes said.

A policeman was standing in the yard. Holmes took a light from him and shone it on the wall.

'Look at this, Watson,' he said.

These words were written on the wall:

'It is the murderer's hand-writing,' Holmes said. 'The same as in the letter that Lestrade showed us.'

'What is happening?' I cried. 'I cannot understand what this killer wants.'

'He wants everybody to be afraid of him,' Holmes told me. 'He wants to be the most evil killer in the world. He had to kill two women tonight, because he did not have time to cut and rip the body of the first. I think he heard somebody coming, and he had to leave the body and run. Then he killed a second time, and cut that woman's body to pieces in the way we have seen.'

We were both silent as the cab took us back to Baker Street, far from the narrow, dirty streets of east London.

I could not sleep that night. Every time I closed my eyes, I saw the body of a woman lying in a dark corner, covered in blood.

Professor Moriarty

Sherlock Holmes was busy with other cases for the next three weeks. There were no new murders in Whitechapel, but people were frightened and angry with the police, who were no nearer to finding the killer than before.

My own life was happy enough. I visited my dear Mary Morstan, and kept this visit a secret from Holmes – something which made me feel unusually clever!

One day Holmes and I had just finished breakfast together.

He was standing by the window, when suddenly he gave a cry.

'What is it, Holmes?' I asked. 'What's the matter?'

He turned towards me. His face was white and the look in his eyes was terrible.

'May I have an hour of your time, Watson?' he asked in a low voice.

'Of course, but . . .'

'Then get your hat and coat.'

He ran out of the house. I followed him quickly and the next two hours passed in a wild chase all over London. We jumped into a cab, out of it again and onto a train, ran down narrow streets and in and out of a big hotel. Finally we came to rest in the peace of a London park.

'You are a true friend, Watson,' Holmes said at last. 'You came with me without a question. Did you realize that someone was following us?'

'I thought so. But who?'

'Can you not guess?'

'No.'

'He calls himself Jack the Ripper.'

'Holmes!' For a moment I found it difficult to speak. Then I asked, 'Did you see him through the window? Where was he?'

'In the empty house opposite ours. He was watching our rooms, Watson. He knows that I am looking for him. We must be very careful. He is one of the most dangerous criminals in Europe.'

'But who is he?' I cried.

'Have you ever heard of Professor Moriarty?'

Two hours passed in a wild chase all over London.

'Never.'

'That is the strangest and most terrible thing about him.' Holmes laughed angrily. 'He is everywhere, but nobody knows him. Like his crimes, he is fantastic.'

I listened in silence as Holmes told me about Moriarty.

'He is an extraordinarily intelligent man. At the age of twenty-one he was a professor of mathematics. For years he was one of the most important men in the world of mathematics. Then he disappeared from university life. Soon after that I began to realize that crime in London was changing. Someone was telling criminals – who are usually stupid and uninteresting little men – what to do. They were obeying the orders of a mastermind. It could only be Moriarty. But I could never catch him. I hate his crimes, but I recognize his intelligence. He is the only criminal who interests me, because he is the only criminal who is as intelligent as I am.

'Then, in August, everything changed. Criminals became stupid again. In the middle of all his success, Moriarty had disappeared. Why?'

'Holmes!' I cried. 'The reason is clear. The Whitechapel murders began in August. It must be . . .'

'No, Watson,' Holmes said. 'It is not clear. Someone like Moriarty does not break locks and climb through windows himself. He gave orders to others. He was the commander-in-chief of the criminal world, not a foot-soldier.'

'Then why . . . I mean, how . . .?'

'Success is too easy for him. He needs change and danger as others need drugs. He was the best at mathematics, then the best at crime. Now he has chosen murder.'

'Do you mean that he kills just to amuse himself?' I asked.

'Yes. He enjoys the danger. But there is another reason. He wishes for a battle with me – the most successful criminal against the most successful detective. It will be a fight to the death.'

'Then these women that he kills . . .'

'They mean nothing to him. He just uses them because they are necessary to his plan.'

'His plan?'

'Yes. I have said that he kills because he is bored and because he wishes for a fight to the death with me. There is a third reason. He wishes to destroy the world we know.'

'He is mad!'

'No. He is not mad. He is evil itself. He wants to bring fear into our lives, to make everyone in London afraid to go out at night, afraid of every sound and shadow. London will become a city of strangers, seeing danger in every neighbour. How can people live like that?'

He was silent for a moment. Then he said, 'I alone can stop him. And stop him I shall.'

Several days later, Inspector Lestrade called to see us again.

'Are you ready to arrest the Whitechapel killer yet?' Holmes asked him.

'We are continuing to make all possible . . .'

'Enough, Lestrade! Have you caught him yet?'

'In a difficult case like this . . .'

'Yes or no?'

'No,' Lestrade said, 'but we hope . . .'

'Of course we hope. We must always hope. But the people of London will not wait for ever for the police to arrest Jack the Ripper. Do you think you could enjoy life as a policeman in Canada, Lestrade?'

Lestrade tried to smile. He said, 'I believe we shall only catch him if we have the luck to find him while he is actually murdering some poor woman.'

He looked surprised when Holmes said, 'That is the first sensible thing I have heard any policeman say about these murders. We must catch him red-handed. A drink, Inspector?'

'Yes, please, Mr Holmes. But who can say when or where he will kill again?'

'I can,' Holmes said coolly. 'Let us look at the dates of the murders. He kills, waits a week, kills again and waits three weeks before the next murder. This changes only when he has, as he tells us, 'no time to rip', and has to kill twice on the same night. The following week there is no murder. I tell you, Lestrade, this is no crazy killer. This is a man who is following a plan. He works only in Whitechapel, and in the early hours of the morning.'

Lestrade looked helplessly at him. 'What shall we do?' he asked.

Holmes jumped to his feet. 'I think he will try to kill again on Monday night. The first murders were on a Friday, a Saturday and a Sunday. He moves a day forward each time. We must close up Whitechapel like a box which he cannot escape from.

'*We must close up Whitechapel like a box.*'

We shall need every policeman you have.'

Lestrade looked worried. 'I'll do what I can, Mr Holmes, but I don't know if my chief will like it.'

'Your chief,' Holmes said, 'will give you all the men you need. I am sure that you will be interested to learn that your chief has asked me to do anything I can to catch this killer. I am free to give you orders, Lestrade, and you are free to obey me.'

When Lestrade had gone, Holmes said, 'Now I need a bath, my dinner and a good sleep. Moriarty wishes to destroy me. He has already, my dear Watson, tried three times to kill me! He is a terrible enemy, and I must get ready for the battle.'

I stared at him in horror, and decided that I would never leave my friend's side while he was in this danger.

Jack the Ripper kills again

On Monday night Whitechapel was full of policemen, all ready to catch Jack the Ripper. Nothing happened. Only Lestrade enjoyed this.

'You have failed, Mr Holmes,' he said. 'Your idea was very clever, but you made one mistake. You forget to tell the murderer about it!'

Holmes and I took a cab back to Baker Street. We were both too tired to talk then, but later that day I said, 'Holmes, what did happen? What went wrong?'

'We did not really fail. Moriarty could not kill anyone because we were there. But I badly wanted to catch him at his work, and there I failed.'

'He was there, then?'

'He was there. He saw what I had done, and realized that he could not kill a woman that night.'

'Then you did not fail! We have beaten him.'

Holmes shook his head slowly.

'No, Watson. We have not beaten him yet. Think how angry he must be! I have stopped him once, and now he will try harder to kill me. He will go on with his planned murders, and he will do everything possible to make sure that he succeeds.'

'But Holmes, how do we . . .?'

'Remember, he kills, waits a week, kills again and then waits three weeks. So he will kill again next weekend. I must talk to Lestrade. But tonight, Watson, we shall amuse ourselves at the theatre.'

He would say no more, but that night, while we were at the theatre, he disappeared from my side without a word. I did not even see him leave, and for several days I neither saw him nor heard from him. Then, at dinner time on the night when we had hoped to catch Jack the Ripper at his work, he suddenly appeared again in Baker Street.

'Holmes!' I cried. 'Where have you been?'

'Don't worry, old fellow.' He sat down by the fire. 'I have been keeping Moriarty busy and playing games with him. He has chased me all over the country, but, as you see, I am still alive. I shall tell you my adventures some other time. Lestrade will be here in a minute to discuss tonight's plan.'

When Lestrade arrived, he did not seem at all pleased to see us.

'So, another of your clever little plans, Mr Holmes,' he said coldly. 'Do you really think we shall see the killer tonight?'

'He will be at work tonight,' Holmes replied. 'The only question is, shall we be ready for him? I suppose you have done everything that I ordered you to do?'

'We are ready for him.'

'Then let us go. We must not keep Jack the Ripper waiting.'

It was a cold, windy night, and we were grateful for our thick coats as we sat in the cab. It took us to the big police station in Commercial Street. Hundreds of policemen were waiting there to begin the night's work. Holmes and I sat down to wait, too.

After some time I said to Holmes, 'This waiting is terrible. I wish we could do something.'

'We can,' he replied.

'When a crime is reported. Until then we can only wait. The murderer could be anywhere out there.'

Holmes picked up a piece of paper and a pencil. 'He could. But I think I know where he is. Look at this.'

This is what he showed me:

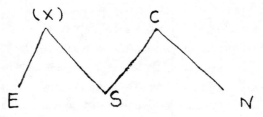

'The letters E, S, C and N are Eddowes, Stride, Chapman and Nicholl, the last four women he has murdered,' Holmes said. 'The diagram shows the place where each died.'

'And X, I suppose, is some unknown woman, the one that he plans to kill tonight,' I said. 'But how do you know where to put the X on your diagram?'

'Look again, Watson,' Holmes said with a smile.

Suddenly, I understood. 'It is a letter M!'

'Yes, Watson. M for murder, M for . . .'

'Moriarty! Holmes, do you mean to say . . .?'

'Yes. He is writing his name in blood upon the face of Whitechapel. And, as you see, I know where he will try to kill tonight, and where I shall go to meet him.'

'Not without me,' I said. 'I must come with you.'

We left the police station just before midnight.

For the first time, I walked through the narrow streets of east London, streets that I had seen before only through the window of a cab. People think that murders happen in dark, empty streets. That is not always true. A strange and horrible fact about the streets where Jack the Ripper murdered women is that they were busier and better lit than most other London streets. They were full of pubs and cheap hotels. At all hours the streets were full of people who were too poor to find a bed anywhere, drunks looking for a bar that never closed, and all kinds of criminals. Finally, there were the women – those women who work only at night, when their more honest sisters are asleep.

I studied medicine in London, and while I was a student I saw something of the low-life of our capital. I was, after all, a healthy

For the first time, I walked through the streets of east London.

young man, and young men must amuse themselves. But I had never seen women like these. Holmes stopped several to question and to warn them, and I looked at their faces carefully. They were old at the age of twenty, dirty, diseased and hopeless. One thing was clear to me – they were not like other women. Does it matter, I began to think, if Jack the Ripper kills women like these? Death by his knife is quick. It cannot be worse than the slow and painful death from disease which most often ends their short lives.

We returned to the police station after one o'clock. I was tired and sick at heart. Lestrade did not stop talking, telling us that we should catch no murderers that night.

Suddenly, Holmes jumped up and walked out into the street. I followed him.

'Stay inside, Watson,' he said. 'You are tired, dear fellow, and you cannot help me.'

'I am coming with you,' I said. 'Nothing will stop me.'

'Come, then. But we must hurry. Moriarty is near. I can feel it.'

It began to rain. He walked fast and I almost had to run to keep up with him. His eyes moved restlessly from side to side. Suddenly he stopped, and stared into the darkness.

'Twice, Watson,' he said softly. 'He will kill twice tonight. We stopped him killing a woman last time, so he must kill two tonight.'

Before I could answer, he was moving again. Then he stopped, and pulled me into a dark corner. Someone was coming towards us. Holmes spoke in a low voice, but I shook with fear at his words.

'It is Moriarty.'

A man passed our corner and disappeared into another street. I could not see his face.

'Run to the police station and fetch Lestrade. He knows what to do,' Holmes said. 'I shall follow Moriarty. Hurry, man, hurry!'

Then he was gone. I cannot explain why I did not do what I was told. The fact is, instead of going to the police station, I followed Holmes. Perhaps I was afraid that my friend could not fight Moriarty on his own.

I ran to the corner of the street. I could just see Moriarty, walking straight on. Then, to my great surprise, Holmes turned left, and disappeared into a house, while Moriarty reached the end of the street and turned the corner. I could not understand what was happening, or what I should do next. What if Holmes, realizing that someone was following him, thought I was one of Moriarty's men? Some minutes later, I was still wondering what to do when I heard a door close. A man came out into the street. It was Holmes. He was now richly dressed, in a hat and a long, dark coat. He had changed his appearance in several small and clever ways, but I knew him.

I wanted to call to him, but was afraid he would not be pleased. Instead, I decided to follow secretly, ready to help him if he needed me.

We walked and walked. The rain became heavier and the streets emptied of people. Then a short fat man passed me, and soon afterwards a girl. She looked like a woman of the streets, but younger and prettier than most I had seen that night. She seemed a little drunk, and could not walk straight.

As she came near to Holmes, he stopped and spoke to her. They both laughed. Further along the street I saw the short fat man, now standing outside a pub, watching them. Then Holmes and the girl walked off together and a few seconds later the man followed them. How I feared for Holmes's safety! I was sure that the man and the girl were working for Moriarty. They had some plan, I knew, to hurt my friend. Perhaps only I could save him.

Holmes and the girl walked on, the man followed them, and I followed all three. At last Holmes and the girl stopped at the entrance to a yard. I heard the woman's voice. I could not hear Holmes's words, but to my surprise I clearly saw him kiss her face. Then they entered the yard, and the fat man crossed the street and went into a house further along. Had he gone to fetch Moriarty, who would now appear and kill my friend?

Slowly and carefully, I made my way into the yard. It was dark, but I could see a light at a window. Then I heard Holmes's voice. He was in that room.

As quietly as I could, I went to the window. The curtains were a little too short, and I could just see into the room. The woman was lying on the bed, drinking from a bottle. Holmes sat with his back to the window, taking snuff from a little silver box. He seemed to be in no danger, but who could say when Moriarty would arrive?

It was cold and wet in the yard, but I felt calm again. If Moriarty came, I was ready to save my friend. I sat down with

As the girl came near to Holmes, he stopped and spoke to her.

my back to the wall to wait.

I am ashamed to say what happened next, but I must say it. I fell asleep. I was asleep for two hours. As I woke up, cold and uncomfortable, Holmes's words came back to me, 'He will kill twice tonight.'

I ran to the window, afraid of what I should see. At first I could not understand what terrible thing had happened there. Was it possible, I wondered, for a person to explode? There was blood everywhere. Then I recognized the body as the woman who I had seen drinking and talking with Sherlock Holmes. He was still with her, but he was not dead. No, much worse than dead. He was alive. He had a knife in his hand, and he was cutting up her face and her body. Even as I watched, he was carefully cutting the leg down to the bone, taking off a long piece of meat in his other hand.

And as he cut the woman to pieces, he was singing.

Moriarty is dead

As a soldier and a doctor, I know that a man who is very badly hurt in battle often feels no pain. If he lives, he remembers nothing about what has happened to him. After that terrible night in Whitechapel, I was like that man. The next day, I woke up and found myself lying in a park. My watch and my money had gone, and I was cold and dirty. I knew that I had spent many

He had a knife in his hand.

hours drinking, but I did not know where I had been, or what had happened to me.

I did not want to go to Baker Street, because I was afraid that Holmes would be there, but I needed a bath and dry clothes. In the end, I paid a cab-driver to knock on the door. The house was empty, so I went in.

There was a telegram from Holmes. 'M has escaped us,' it said. 'He is trying to leave the country, but I am following him.'

I did not know what to think. Was I mad, or was my best friend, the man who I had worked with for so many years, a murderer?

That evening, the murder in Whitechapel of a young woman called Mary Kelly was reported in the newspapers. This murder was more bloody, more horrible than any that had happened before. It was clear that it was the work of Jack the Ripper.

I was still reading the newspaper reports of the murder when Lestrade arrived.

'Good evening, doctor,' he said. 'I'd like a word with Mr Holmes.'

I did not know what to say. Did the police already know what Holmes had done?

Then Lestrade saw the telegram, picked it up and read it. 'Running off for a little holiday, is he?' he said. 'Some of us have to work for a living. We've had enough of Mr Holmes and the kind of help he gives the police.'

'Come now,' I said. 'Holmes was right. There was a murder on the night he told us that there would be.'

Lestrade laughed. 'Oh yes. There was a murder all right. We had hundreds of policemen on the streets, but we couldn't stop the murder or catch the killer. The police were everywhere – except the little corner of Whitechapel where the girl died.'

He spoke in a low voice as he continued, 'I've never seen anything like it. It will be days before I can eat meat again.

You're lucky you didn't see her, doctor. We had to keep the worst thing of all out of the newspapers, but I can tell *you*. The girl was pregnant. He cut her up, and he cut up the baby, too.'

I felt a cold hand touch me. 'He will kill twice tonight.'

'What did you say?'

'Oh, nothing. What are you doing to catch him?'

'What can we do? Nobody heard a scream or saw anything.' He looked again at the telegram. 'Who is this "M"?' he asked.

'Oh, he just means the murderer,' I said.

After Lestrade left, I tried hard to think of some other way of explaining what I had seen that night. I had seen Holmes cutting up the body, but I had not seen him kill the girl. How could my dear friend possibly be this terrible killer? Perhaps it was all part of some clever plan that I did not understand.

For some days I thought I had found an answer to the problem, but then a telegram arrived from Holmes, who was now in Switzerland. It said, 'M is no more. Returning Saturday. Holmes.'

Suddenly I realized that I was afraid of seeing him again, and my worry returned, stronger than ever. Was he the killer or not? I had to know the truth – and quickly. To help me think clearly, I wrote down what I knew.

Is Sherlock Holmes the Whitechapel murderer?

The arguments for:

1 He was in Whitechapel on the nights of the murders, and alone at the right times.

2 When he was out of London or I was with him, there were no murders.

3 He can change his appearance easily.

4 He studied medicine. He could easily cut up a body in the dark.

5 He knows the lanes and yards of Whitechapel well.

6 He can escape from the police because he knows their plans – indeed, he makes their plans.

The arguments against:

1 He spends his life fighting crime.

2 I know my friend. I know he could not do these things.

When I read what I had written, I began to wonder how well I knew Holmes. Did he really fight against crime? He took cases because they interested him, not because he hated crime. It was all just a game to him. He fought crime to amuse himself.

It was now late at night. I was terribly tired, but I knew that I had to decide what to do before Holmes came back. Suddenly, as I lay back in my chair, half-asleep, the terrible picture of Holmes cutting up that girl's body appeared again before my eyes. Then, finally, I knew. It was not *what* I had seen him do, but *how* he had done it. That look of cool amusement on his face. The way he sang as he worked. The man who could do that could do anything.

Next day I packed my bags and moved into a hotel. That evening I asked Mary to have dinner with me. I told her that I could not sleep while she lived alone in London and the Whitechapel murderer was free to kill again. I asked her to marry me sooner than we had planned. She laughed and said she was not afraid of the murderer. He never killed women like her. But she would marry me as soon as possible, she said, because I

I had to decide what to do before Holmes came back.

looked so worried and unhappy.

Then I wrote a letter to Holmes.

'I am sorry that I cannot welcome you home,' I wrote, 'but I have a reason for that, the best reason in the world. Mary and I are married. She was badly frightened by those awful murders in Whitechapel and will feel safer now that I am by her side.

'It is wonderful to hear from you that Professor Moriarty is dead. Of course I look forward to hearing the full story of his death from you.

'Mary and I are spending a little time travelling. Please write to me at my London club.'

Several days later, Mary and I were married, and we left London. In a quiet little town by the sea, with Mary by my side, I felt strong enough to face the awful truth about Holmes, and to think about what I had to do. I could not go to the police with my story. They would think that I was mad. I decided that I would have to watch Holmes carefully. Only I could stop him killing again.

When I returned to London, I found a letter from Holmes waiting for me at my club. He told me that he was going to Russia, to work on a strange and exciting murder case.

'I am bored with London, now that Jack the Ripper is dead,' he wrote. 'Perhaps the foreign criminal has more to offer me. I shall not return to London for some time. Please inform me of your new address.'

After reading this, I was happier than I had been for many

weeks. Mary and I finished our holiday and moved to a house in London, not far from Baker Street. I was busy with my work as a doctor, and we lived quietly and happily together.

During this time I was sent two wonderful letters by Holmes. He had brought his work on the Russian mystery to a successful end, and had gone from Russia to Ceylon, where the sudden death of a rich tea-planter offered him the interest and excitement he needed. The Holmes who wrote these letters to me sounded like the old Holmes that I knew.

'He is dangerous when he is bored and uses cocaine,' I thought. 'When he is enjoying his work, London is safe.'

One day in March, as I walked along Baker Street, I saw a light in Holmes's window, and knew that he had returned. I went in, and he welcomed me like the dear old friend he had been. All evening we sat by the fire, and he told me everything that had happened in Russia and Ceylon. But what I really wanted to hear about was Moriarty's death, and about that he said not one word.

At last I could wait no longer.

'My dear Holmes,' I said. 'It is almost midnight, and you still have not told me how Moriarty died!'

At once his face went white, and his eyes became fixed in a stare. He sat silent and unmoving, as the seconds passed.

Then he said, 'I'm sorry, Watson. I was thinking about something to do with my last case. What did you say?'

'Moriarty,' I repeated. 'You have not told me how he died.'

'He has gone,' he said. 'That is all that anyone needs to know about him.'

'He has gone,' Holmes said. 'That is all that
anyone needs to know.'

I asked him to tell me more, and found out that his final meeting with Moriarty had been in Switzerland, on a narrow path above a famous waterfall. Holmes had won the argument, he told me coldly. And that was all that he would tell me.

Holmes and I were friends again, and soon I began helping him with new cases. It was just like old times. I am afraid that I often left my wife alone, and I did not give enough time to my patients, but I was happy to see Holmes interested and busy.

One day he gave me his cocaine-bottle. 'Take it, doctor,' he said. 'I do not need it any more.'

I was very pleased indeed at this news, and only one thing that happened at this time worried me. A woman was killed in Whitechapel, and people began to talk again about Jack the Ripper. I carefully checked where Holmes had been on the night of the murder, and found that he had spent the evening with two famous foreign detectives. I even spoke to them both secretly, and so I was sure that Holmes had not been in Whitechapel that night.

In 1890 I decided that I must begin to spend less time with Holmes. I wanted to be a success as a doctor, and I knew that I was not working hard enough for that. Mary and I moved to a new house, further from Baker Street.

There was another change, too. ACD's story, *A Study in Scarlet*, which had failed in this country, was a big success in America, and he began to write about more of Holmes's cases. To my surprise, Holmes quickly agreed to let him do this. He had been angry when he first read *A Study in Scarlet,* but now he seemed amused by what ACD was doing.

1891 began, and life for me was calm and happy. I was working hard, and I had little time to spend with Holmes. Jack the Ripper was a thing of the past, as forgotten as yesterday's newspapers, as dead as the women he had murdered. But Jack was not dead. He was only resting, and his rest would soon be over.

Death at the Reichenbach Falls

In February 1891 a woman called Flora White was killed with a knife in Whitechapel. Everyone thought that the murderer was Jack the Ripper. I alone knew that this was not true. I was sure that 'Jack' had not killed the last two women to die on the streets of Whitechapel.

Soon after this, Holmes left for France. He sent me a strange letter from there which worried me very much. I could not understand a word of it and began to wonder if he was taking cocaine again. This was his letter:

If you remember the Berlin case of 'one in three', Watson, everything will be clear to you because . . . *the famous German professor in Paris is no longer alive. I heard he was recently killed while studying flora in the White Mountains of my favourite island. Letters and books are appearing soon. Read them quickly but carefully, as I cannot always follow or understand him myself. Last night I dreamt and the next day suddenly understood this problem. The time comes when he and others will be free – not an easy escape.*

About three weeks after that, I was sitting alone at home one evening. My wife was away on a visit. Suddenly, the door opened, and Holmes came in. He then ran to the window, closed it and locked it.

'Holmes,' I cried. 'What has happened? You look terrible!'

He looked old and ill, and he was shaking with tiredness.

'What is it?' I asked. 'Are you afraid of something?'

'Of someone,' he said. 'Did you not get my letter?'

'Yes, but I didn't understand it. What is wrong?'

Holmes looked at me sadly. 'You didn't understand it. Is your wife here?'

'No, she is away. Do you want to sleep here? I shall make sure that you are in no danger.'

He shook his head. 'I cannot rest anywhere. If I sleep, he will win! I cannot stay here. I would bring evil into your house. But you can help me, Watson. I must leave the country tomorrow. Will you come with me?'

'Where are you going, Holmes?'

'Going? I am not going anywhere. I am trying to escape from him. But he will find me again. Everywhere I go, he will follow me.'

'Who is he, Holmes?' I asked.

'Professor Moriarty, of course!'

'But Moriarty is dead,' I said.

'What has happened? You look terrible!'

'Dead!' he screamed. 'He is trying to kill me! How can he be dead?'

'But you told me that he was dead.'

'I was mistaken,' Holmes said. 'He is not dead. I told you that.'

'You told me? But when? Where?'

'In my letter, man! The Berlin case – every third word! A very easy hidden message, Watson. I thought even you . . . Oh, it doesn't matter. The fact is, Moriarty is alive and free in London. He killed a woman only three weeks ago. He will kill again if I do not stop him. It is a fight to the death between us. Come with me and help me, Watson. Say that you will come!'

'Of course I will come, old fellow,' I said.

He smiled and lay back in the chair. In a second, he was asleep. Quickly, I gave him an injection to keep him asleep. Then, with the help of my cook, I put him to bed and locked the bedroom door. After that I had a drink and sat down to think about what I must do.

Perhaps I did not understand Holmes's hidden messages, but I did understand what was happening to the man. He was mad – I knew that now. All that was evil in him he called Moriarty. The fight with Moriarty was a battle that was taking place inside his own head.

I had hoped that Jack the Ripper was dead. He was not, and now another woman had been murdered. I felt that her blood was on my hands. The time had come when I must tell Holmes what I knew about him. First, I had to be sure that I understood everything.

I took a cab to Baker Street, and went into Holmes's rooms. I did not know what I was looking for, but I began to search. The rooms were untidy, full of old newspapers. I searched for four hours but found nothing. At four o'clock in the morning I stopped. I went to the window and looked out at the dark sky.

Suddenly, I knew what to do. The house opposite, where Holmes had once seen Moriarty. I ran across the street and broke the lock on the back door of the house. Every room was empty, all except one bedroom. This contained a bed, a cupboard and a box full of papers. All the papers were about the Whitechapel murders. Some were cut from newspapers, others were written by the killer himself. He described each murder with a sick enjoyment of what he had done.

Under the papers I found some glass jars of the kind that are used in hospitals. In them were pieces of women's bodies. In the last jar was the worst thing of all – pieces of the body of a little unborn child.

When I saw that, all the friendly feelings I had ever had for Sherlock Holmes died inside me. Now I could go straight to Lestrade and ask him to arrest Holmes, but I chose not to do that. I did not want all England to know what Holmes, once a good and wise man, had become. Some evil things are best hidden from the world. I, and I alone, would face him and his crimes.

I went out into the cold morning air. I felt strangely calm, but also excited.

Holmes was still asleep. I searched his clothes for drugs and guns, but found only a little money and his silver snuffbox. Then

All the papers were about the Whitechapel murders.

I wrote a letter to Lestrade. I told my cook to take it to my bank manager. If I failed to return, I asked him to send it to Lestrade. In the letter I told Lestrade everything that I knew about Sherlock Holmes and the Whitechapel murders.

I was very tired, but I knew that I had to stay awake. I had to watch Holmes all the time. I decided to use the cocaine he had given me. I added water to the drug and put it into a medicine bottle. Then I injected some into my arm.

It was time to look in on Holmes. As I opened the door, I saw that his bed was empty. He was behind the door. He tried to hit me, but the drug made me quick, and I jumped out of the way.

'Watson!' he cried. 'Dear fellow! I thought you were Moriarty. One of his men is in your garden. We must go now! It is too dangerous to stay here!'

The man who he had seen was William, my gardener.

'I will go and pack,' I said.

'No luggage! He must not know what we are doing!'

'Let me take my doctor's bag,' I said. 'He will think that I am going to visit a patient.'

'Excellent!' Holmes said. 'I had the same idea myself.'

He did not know that I had packed the cocaine, money and a gun in my doctor's bag.

Holmes sent me out before him to find a cab. We drove through the streets, jumped out of the cab, ran some way, and found another cab. But at the station, Holmes said, 'Moriarty is here. He has followed us. We must change trains as soon as we can.'

We jumped from the moving train, ran across fields, caught

another train, and at last took the night boat from Newhaven. For five days we travelled through France and Germany in the same wild and crazy way. Holmes would not say where we were going. I never took my eyes off him during those days, but the right moment to talk to him never came. Holmes seemed stronger than ever, while I was getting weaker every day. Only the cocaine made it possible for me to stay awake.

Finally, sitting one night in a hotel in Switzerland, I knew that I could not go on much longer. I had told Holmes that next day I wanted to walk over the mountains to the famous Reichenbach Falls. I decided that I would tell him what I knew about him when we were alone in the mountains. The cocaine was almost finished. Whether I lived or died, the end must come that day.

We did not begin our walk to the Reichenbach Falls until the afternoon. Holmes refused to go out before lunch. I was frightened. I had no more cocaine, and soon I would be too tired to go on. At last we left the hotel, and started to walk along the mountain paths. Holmes talked happily as we went. He found the mountains very beautiful.

When we had gone a little way, I found that I had left my watch at the hotel. It had belonged to my father, and I wanted to know that it was safe. I told Holmes that I would return to the hotel, find the watch, and see him later at the Falls. I hoped that I was doing the right thing, and that he would not disappear.

When at last I reached the Falls, I could not see him, and thought for a moment that he had escaped me. Then I saw a narrow path which was cut into the rock right above the Falls themselves. Holmes was standing on that path, watching the water crash down onto the rocks. There was nowhere he could run to. It could not be easier for me.

I moved towards him. Suddenly he turned and our eyes met. His look was cool, untroubled. How could I hope to frighten this man? My heart failed me and I almost fell. He stepped forward to help me, but I pulled out my gun.

'Back!' I shouted. 'Another step and I shall shoot!'

He smiled. 'Very well, doctor. I understand.'

My hands shook and I almost dropped the gun. 'It's over, Holmes,' I said. 'I've been to the empty house. I know everything.'

He laughed. 'Dear fellow! Nobody knows everything!'

I seemed to hear voices coming to me from the water, and I could now see two Holmeses – one on the path and one standing on air.

'I've found the jars, Holmes, and the papers. I know you killed them.'

'I killed them? Which? The jars or the papers?'

Nothing seemed real. It was getting harder and harder for me to speak. Holmes watched me, smiling.

'I know you did it, Holmes,' I shouted. 'I watched you cut Mary Kelly to pieces. You killed them! Let me hear you say that you did!'

'What is it you want me to say?'

'Say you killed them!'

'You killed them.'

'I am going to shoot you, Holmes!' I screamed. 'Before you die, tell me that you understand what you have done!'

49

'I am going to shoot you, Holmes!' I screamed.

'You're mad, doctor,' he said. 'And you're talking rubbish. Go on, shoot me!'

I shot him. I shot again and again, but still he stood there.

Finally, I fell to the ground. I could not move. It seemed a long time before I could say, 'Why aren't you dead?'

I stared up at him as he stood above me, calmly inhaling snuff from his snuffbox.

'I took the bullets from your gun and put in blanks,' he said conversationally. 'Tell me, Moriarty, when did you kill Watson? You are very clever. You look almost like him, but I know who you are. When I saw you injecting cocaine three times a day, I knew then for sure that you were not my dear friend. Dr Watson would never, never take drugs. Your cocaine is finished, isn't it? Poor Moriarty! Did you not realize that my snuffbox contains cocaine, not snuff?'

I felt sick and weak. Before my eyes Holmes was changing colour – red, then green, then blue. I shook my head to clear it, but he was still talking.

'And your letter, telling Lestrade that I was the Whitechapel murderer. What rubbish! How Scotland Yard would laugh! But I have the letter here – I saw it in your cook's hand and took it from her while you were calling the cab. You have failed, Moriarty. I have enjoyed making you run around Europe with me, but now you must die.'

He took out a long knife.

'Holmes!' I cried. 'I am Watson, your friend, Watson! I have tried to save you – save you from yourself and from the police!'

He held up the knife and stepped towards me.

'If you kill me,' I screamed, 'Moriarty will win! That is what he wants! Kill your only friend, and Moriarty has won!'

I closed my eyes and waited for the pain and the darkness.

It did not come. I opened my eyes and saw that Holmes was looking at me. He had put the knife down. The look in his eyes was sadder than anything that I had ever seen. He seemed to see far into both the past and the future, and to find them sad beyond words.

'Never fear, old fellow,' he said. 'I shall not let him hurt you.'

Then he stepped backwards off the path. I saw his body hit the rocks far below.

'I shall not let him hurt you,' Holmes said.

Conclusion

Two days later I woke up. I was in bed at the hotel. Someone had found me on the edge of the path, high above the Reichenbach Falls.

After a week I returned to London. I went immediately to the empty house, where I burned the papers and destroyed the jars. I wanted to be sure that nobody would ever know the evil things that Holmes had done. I wanted only the good that was in my friend to live on after his death.

I was lucky. ACD had been busy writing more stories about Holmes. These stories were an immediate success. ACD became a famous writer, and people who had never met Holmes the man, knew Holmes the story-book detective. As the years passed, people began to forget that Sherlock Holmes had ever been a real person.

After Holmes's death my life was difficult for a long time. It was two years before I could live without cocaine. I could not work, and my wife and I had little money.

My story is at an end. Since Holmes's death I have lived quietly. But sometimes, as I sit by the fire in the evening, I think of that day at the Reichenbach Falls. I hear again the gentleness of Holmes's last words, and see the light of understanding in his eyes during those last moments, when he seemed once again the best and wisest man I have ever known.

Sometimes I think of that day at the Reichenbach Falls.

Exercises

A Checking your understanding

Foreword and Introduction *How much can you remember? Check your answers.*

1 In which year was the box that contained Dr Watson's story opened?
2 What was ACD's job before he became a writer?
3 What was the name of the first Sherlock Holmes story that ACD wrote?
4 Who agreed to become Dr Watson's wife?

Chapter 1 *Find answers to these questions in the text.*

1 Why did Sherlock Holmes become unhappy and bored?
2 What was especially horrible about the Whitechapel murders?
3 What plan did the police have for catching the murderer?
4 What did the murderer write on the wall by the body of one woman that he killed?

Chapter 2 *Are these sentences true (T) or false (F)?*

1 Holmes told Watson that Jack the Ripper was really Professor Moriarty.
2 Moriarty was a professor of medicine.
3 He became a murderer because he hated women.
4 Holmes said that he knew when Moriarty would kill again.

Chapter 3 *Write answers to these questions.*

1 When Holmes saw Moriarty in the streets of Whitechapel, what did he ask Watson to do?
2 What did Holmes do to the girl which surprised Watson?
3 Why didn't Watson see who killed the girl?
4 What was Holmes doing as he cut up the girl's body?

Chapter 4 *Are these sentences true (T) or false (F)?*

1 After the murder of Mary Kelly, Watson did not see Holmes for a long time.
2 Watson began to feel sure that Holmes was Jack the Ripper.

3 Watson married Mary sooner than planned because she was afraid of Jack the Ripper.

4 Holmes wanted to tell Watson how Moriarty had died.

Chapter 5 and Conclusion *Write answers to these questions.*

1 Why was Holmes frightened when he came to Watson's house?

2 What did Watson find in the empty house opposite Holmes's rooms in Baker Street?

3 How did Watson stay awake during his last journey with Holmes?

4 Why did Holmes want to kill Watson?

5 How did Holmes die?

6 Why was Sherlock Holmes remembered long after his death?

B Working with language

1 *Put together these beginnings and endings of sentences. Check your answers in the Foreword, Introduction and Chapter 1.*

1 Dr Watson was seventy-three

2 Watson had known Holmes for almost four years

3 Holmes began to use cocaine

4 The murderer had to kill a second woman

5 Watson liked *A Study in Scarlet*

6 Lestrade came to Holmes

7 Watson told Holmes to stop using cocaine

8 Holmes went to Whitechapel

9 to ask for his help.

10 but Holmes only laughed at him.

11 when he died.

12 to live among the poor people there.

13 when he met ACD.

14 because he was bored.

15 but Holmes hated it.

16 because he had no time to cut up the first one.

2 *Complete these sentences with information from Chapter 4.*

1 After he saw Holmes cutting up the girl's body, Watson did not want to go to Baker Street because . . .

2 When Lestrade saw the telegram from Holmes, he . . .

3 Watson asked Mary to . . .

4 Holmes wrote to Watson at his club, to tell him that . . .

5 When Holmes returned to London, Watson wanted to know . . .

6 By 1891 everyone thought that Jack the Ripper was dead, but . . .

C Activities

1 What kind of man was Dr Watson? Write a few lines about him.

2 You are a newspaper reporter. Write a report about the murder of Mary
Kelly.

3 Write out the hidden message in the strange letter which Holmes sent to
Watson from France. Now try to write another hidden message, using
every third word, from Watson to his wife, just after Holmes's death.
Do you know, or can you make up, any other ways of sending a hidden
message?

4 You are one of the people in 1976 who did not believe Watson's story.
Write an angry letter to a newspaper, and say that Watson was lying or
he was sick, and that it was impossible for the great Sherlock Holmes to
be the Whitechapel murderer.

Glossary

blank blanks in a gun make a loud noise when the gun is fired, but no bullets come out

cab an old kind of taxi, which was pulled by horses

case a crime which is a problem for the police

city a large and important town

club a building used by the club members where they can stay, have meals, read the newspapers, etc.

cocaine a dangerous drug which is usually taken through the nose, as a white powder

commander-in-chief the head of an army

curtains pieces of cloth hung up in front of windows

diagram a drawing or plan that explains something

drug a dangerous medicine (e.g. cocaine) which some people take to get excitement and to make them feel different

drunk (*adj* and *n*) a person who has drunk too much alcohol

evil (*adj* and *n*) very bad

falls (*n*) a waterfall; a place where a river falls from a high place to a lower place

fellow (*informal*) a man

flora all the plants of a particular area

great large or very important

horrible frightening, terrible

horror great fear or dislike

inject to put medicine or a drug into the body with a special needle

injection putting medicine or a drug into the body with a needle

inhale to breathe in through the nose

jar a container or pot, usually made of glass

kiss to touch someone, usually someone you like or love, with your lips

lane a narrow street

mad crazy, with a sick mind

mastermind someone very intelligent, who plans other people's work (or crimes)

mathematics the science of numbers

path a narrow way for people to walk on

patient (*n*) a sick person who goes to a doctor for medical help

pregnant expecting a baby

professor the highest level of teacher in a university

red-handed (catch someone) catch someone in the middle of doing something wrong

rip (*v*) to cut violently with a knife

Ripper (*n*) a name given to a murderer who cuts people up

safety being safe, out of danger

scarlet bright red

Scotland Yard the headquarters of the London police

snuff tobacco, as a powder which is taken in through the nose

stare (*n* and *v*) to look very hard at something

telegram a quick way of sending a message by electric wires or radio

truth the facts; what is true, what really happened

waterfall a place where a river falls from a high place to a lower place

weak not strong

wise knowing many things; knowing what is right and good

yard a piece of hard ground with buildings all round it

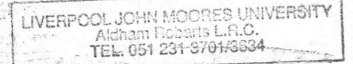